The Snowball War

by Bernice Chardiet and Grace Maccarone
pictures by G. Brian Karas

SCHOLASTIC INC.
New York Toronto London Auckland Sydney

To Nancy, Karen, Beth, and Tara
G.M.

To Ron Myrtis and Shari,
who know a lot about snow
B.C.

To Richy, Megan, and Michael
G.B.K.

ISBN 0-590-44933-8

Copyright © 1992 by Grace Maccarone and Chardiet Unlimited, Inc.

All rights reserved. Published by Scholastic Inc.

12 11 10 9 8 7 6 5 4 3   2 3 4 5 6/9

Printed in the U.S.A.   08

First Scholastic printing, January 1992

Bunny wanted to play in the snow all day.
But she had to go to school.

Bunny made footprints in the snow.
First she made a straight line.

Then she made a squiggle.

Thud!
Something hit the back
of Bunny's coat.
It was a snowball.

Bunny turned around.
No one was there.

Bunny saw her friend, Cynthia,
in the schoolyard.

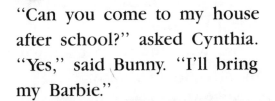

"Can you come to my house
after school?" asked Cynthia.
"Yes," said Bunny. "I'll bring
my Barbie."
"You're my best friend in the
whole world," Cynthia said.

Raymond was waiting for them
in the classroom.
"I know who threw that snowball,"
Raymond said to Bunny.
"Who?" Bunny asked.
"It was me," said Raymond.
The school bell rang.

"It's time to take your seats. We have
lots to do today," said Ms. Darcy.
The class worked hard all morning.

At recess, Ms. Darcy's class played
"The Farmer in the Dell."
Sammy was the farmer,
and Brenda was the farmer's wife.
Brenda picked Cynthia to be the child.

"...The Farmer picks the wife..."

Then Cynthia picked Bunny to be the nurse.
Bunny liked having a best friend!

"Farmer in the Dell..."

Raymond was the rat as usual. Raymond Allen Tally's initials spelled R.A.T., which was what most of the kids called him.

R.A.T. picked Martin to be the cheese.

After "The Farmer in the Dell,"
the kids jumped rope.
It was Bunny's turn.
She looked over at Cynthia.

Brenda was whispering in Cynthia's ear.
And she was pointing at Bunny.
Bunny wondered why.
Her feet got tangled in the rope.
Cynthia and Brenda giggled.

"What's so funny?" Bunny asked.
"It's a secret," Brenda said.
"Yes, it's a secret," Cynthia repeated.
"And we won't tell you."
"That's not fair," said Bunny. "You're
supposed to be my best friend."

When Ms. Darcy blew her whistle
the boys and girls lined up and
went back to their classroom.

It was still snowing after school.
"I'll get my Barbie, and then I'll be
right over," Bunny said to Cynthia.
"I changed my mind," Cynthia said.
"You can't come over today.
I'm going to Brenda's house."

Bunny was very sad as she walked home.
Cynthia and Brenda walked ahead of her.
They were holding hands and giggling.
"Look at Brenda," Bunny thought to herself.
"She thinks she's a princess with those curls
bobbing up and down."

Bunny felt a snowball hit her.
She turned around and saw R.A.T.
"Why do I have all the bad luck?"
Bunny wondered.

On Saturday Bunny went outside
to play in the snow.
Cynthia and Brenda were already
playing in Brenda's yard.
"Hi, Bunny!" Brenda waved.
"Come over and play with us."
Bunny was happy that the girls wanted
to play with her again.

"Hi, Bunny," Cynthia said.
Brenda whispered in Bunny's ear.
"Cynthia is a sore loser. I don't
like playing with her anymore.
Let's hide from her."

Suddenly, Cynthia found herself all alone.
"Where are you?" she called.

Cynthia searched and searched.
She could not find Brenda or
Bunny anywhere.

Cynthia started to cry.
"They don't like me anymore," she said.
And she slowly walked home.

At lunchtime, Cynthia called
Bunny on the telephone.
"Let's be best friends again,"
Cynthia said.
"Brenda is too bossy," Bunny said.
"Let's not play with her," said Cynthia.

"Can you come over?" Bunny said.
"I'll be right there," said Cynthia.

Bunny and Cynthia were making
snow angels when Brenda walked by.
"If you play with Cynthia, you can't
play with me," Brenda said to Bunny.
"We don't want to play with you,"
said Bunny.
"See if I care," said Brenda.

She walked back to her yard
and made snow angels of her own.

Just then Bunny and Cynthia were
both hit by snowballs.
When they looked up, they saw R.A.T.,
Sammy, and Martin.
The boys were safe behind a snow fort.

"A snowball fight!" Bunny yelled.
Bunny and Cynthia ran behind a bush.

Cynthia didn't have good aim.
So Cynthia made the snowballs,
while Bunny threw them.

"We're outnumbered," Cynthia said.
"We need help."
"Brenda's good at throwing snowballs,"
said Bunny. "Should we ask her?"
"Yes," said Cynthia. "I hope she'll come."
"Brenda!" Bunny hollered.
"We need your help!"

Brenda ran over to Bunny and Cynthia.
She had to dodge snowballs all the way.

"You sure do need my help," Brenda said.
Brenda had a strong throwing arm.
First she got R.A.T. Then she got Sammy.
Then she got R.A.T. again.

But the boys were still winning.
They had a giant pile of snowballs.
They didn't have to stop to make more.

"They must have a million snowballs,"
Brenda said.
"They must have been making them
all morning," said Bunny.
"They must have been making them
all week," said Cynthia.

"I have a plan," Brenda said.
"You two stay here. I'll sneak up on
the boys and smash their snowballs!"

Bunny and Cynthia kept throwing.
But it was hard to keep up with the
three boys and all their snowballs.

Then the snowballs stopped coming.
"I did it!" Brenda shouted.
"I destroyed their snowballs."
"You didn't get this one," R.A.T. said.
"I have one more just for you."

As R.A.T. threw the last snowball
at Brenda, she ducked.
The snowball hit Martin.
"Whose side are you on?"
Martin asked R.A.T.

"Let's all be on the same side,"
said Bunny. "Let's all be friends."
"I have an idea," said Martin.
"Let's go to my house for hot chocolate."

And that's what they did.